SOME OF MY BEST FRIENDS ARE POLKA-DOT PIGS

BY SARA ANDERSON

I WOULD LIKE TO THANK MY FRIENDS—FOR MANY REASONS, KATHY, ROSE, CLAIRE & CHARLIE, MY EDITOR, AND A VERY SPECIAL THANK YOU TO MARSHALL, WHO BROUGHT THE ANTS.

TYPOGRAPHY: BERNARDO PEBENITO
ART CAPTURE: ART IMAGING
COLOR SEPARATIONS: DIGITAL IMAGE INC.

FIRST EDITION PUBLISHED 1996.
SECOND EDITION PUBLISHED 2000, 2010
BY SARA ANDERSON CHILDREN'S BOOKS
SEATTLE, WASHINGTON
WWW.SARANDERSON.COM

PRINTED IN CHINA
ISBN 978-0-9702784-0-1
2 4 6 8 10 9 7 5 3

LP6.10-1

"THE END IS NOTHING;
THE ROAD IS ALL."

—WILLA SIBERT CATHER

TO
TOUTE-TOUTE
AND ALL
OUR FRIENDS

HI!

SOME OF MY BEST FRIENDS ARE POLKA-DOT PIGS

SOME OF MY BEST FRIENDS ARE WHIRLIGIGS

SOME OF MY BEST FRIENDS EAT PURPLE DAISIES

SOME OF MY BEST FRIENDS ARE MOPPETY MAISIES

POLKA POLKA POLKA-DOT WHIRLY PURPLE MAISIE

SOME OF MY BEST FRIENDS WEAR MANY HATS

SOME OF MY BEST FRIENDS ARE THE WACKIEST BATS

SOME OF MY BEST FRIENDS ARE BIRDS THAT CAN'T FLY

SOME OF MY BEST FRIENDS ARE HYENAS THAT CRY

MANY HATS WACKY BATS CAN'T FLY DON'T CRY

POLKA POLKA POLKA-DOT WHIRLY PURPLE MAISIE

SOME OF MY BEST FRIENDS
ALWAYS WEAR RED

SOME OF MY BEST FRIENDS SPEND ALL DAY IN BED

SOME OF MY BEST FRIENDS EAT PORCUPINE PIE

SOME OF MY BEST FRIENDS ARE IN LOVE WITH THE SKY

DRESS IN RED STAY IN BED PORCUPINE SKY

MANY HATS WACKY BATS
CAN'T FLY DON'T CRY
POLKA POLKA POLKA-DOT
WHIRLY PURPLE MAISIE

SOME OF MY BEST FRIENDS HAVE PINEAPPLE FEET

SOME OF MY BEST FRIENDS
AREN'T VERY NEAT

SOME OF MY BEST FRIENDS ARE LITTLE TINY ANTS

SOME OF MY BEST FRIENDS WEAR BIG BAGGY PANTS

STICKY FEET CAN'T BE NEAT
MARCHING ANTS CLIMB YOUR PANTS
DRESS IN RED STAY IN BED
PORCUPINE SKY

MANY HATS WACKY BATS
CAN'T FLY DON'T CRY
POLKA POLKA POLKA-DOT
WHIRLY PURPLE MAISIE

PURPLE OR POLKA-DOT
WACKY OR SHY
I LOVE MY BEST FRIENDS
THEY ARE THE STARS
IN MY SKY

A SPARKLE A DANCE
A MOON AND A STAR
IN A WORLD FULL OF LUCKY
TO BE LOVED AS WE ARE